WESTMINSTER SCHOOLS

PRESENTED BY

A friend

Lindsy Reed

SMYTHE
GAMBRELL
LIBRARY

MARATHON
AND STEVE

❖

Mary Rayner

E. P. DUTTON ❖ NEW YORK

for Don

Also by Mary Rayner

Mr. and Mrs. Pig's Evening Out
Garth Pig and the Icecream Lady
Mrs. Pig's Bulk Buy
Crocodarling
Mrs. Pig Gets Cross and Other Stories

Copyright © 1989 by Mary Rayner
All rights reserved.
Library of Congress Cataloging-in-Publication Data
Rayner, Mary.   Marathon and Steve/Mary Rayner.—1st ed.
p.   cm.
Summary: Marathon the dog has difficulty sharing his master's
enthusiasm for their daily run. Then an injury suggests an
alternative form of exercise.
ISBN 0-525-44456-4
[1. Dogs—Fiction.   2. Running—Fiction.]   I. Title.
PZ7.R2315Mar   1989   88-18912
[E]—dc19   CIP
                                                        AC
Published in the United States by
E. P. Dutton, New York, N.Y.,
a division of NAL Penguin Inc.
Published simultaneously in Canada by
Fitzhenry & Whiteside Limited, Toronto
Editor: Ann Durell
Printed in Hong Kong by South China Printing Co.
First Edition   10 9 8 7 6 5 4 3 2 1

There was once a dog called Marathon. His owner called him that because his owner liked running.

His owner's name was Steve,
and he ran to keep in shape.
He ran in the mornings and
he ran in the evenings...

he ran along town roads and
he ran along country roads...

he ran uphill
and he ran downhill.
He was in excellent shape.

Marathon hated running.
He didn't even like walking.
All dogs like walks, people
will tell you. Not Marathon.
He liked eating...

he liked lying by the fire...

and he liked watching television.

"Come on, Marathon," said Steve one afternoon, putting on his shoes. "Time for a run."

Marathon looked up but did not move. Inside, he thought about the hard pavement and the cold autumn wind. His heart sank, and he whined.

"You're whining to get out into the fresh air, *I* know," said Steve. "Wait a second," and he jogged up and down in the hall to loosen up.

Marathon tried to prick up his ears and look eager. It was what other dogs did, he knew. He had seen them on television. But however hard he tried, his ears just would not prick up. It's no good, he thought, I'm not a real dog. I just hate walks.

Off went Steve, springing along towards the park,
and after him came Marathon, plonking down one
big paw after another in an effort to keep up. Fresh
air, thought Marathon. Ha!

Up in the park the wind blew Marathon's ears inside out and cut through his fur.

He stopped to sniff at an interesting smell, but Steve whistled at him.

"Come on, Marathon,"
he shouted. "No lagging
behind."

Marathon lumbered forward.

Steve ran along the road and across to the far side of the park.

Marathon followed.

Steve ran past the big school and downhill
to the street market.

Marathon followed.

Steve ran to the far end of the market, under the railway bridge and out of sight.

Marathon followed.

When he reached the railway bridge, he could not see Steve at all, so he put his nose down and trailed him. Then he saw him, sitting on the sidewalk in the middle of a small crowd. Steve was holding one foot and his face was white.

Marathon spurted forward, ears flying and tongue
hanging out, and arrived in a flurry.

He jumped up and licked Steve's face, but Steve pushed him down. Marathon wondered what was wrong.

Then two men helped Steve up, but he could not stand on one of his feet, let alone walk on it. Marathon could sense that it was hurting him a lot.

Just then a police car drove by. The policemen saw
the crowd and stopped. When he found out what
had happened, one of the policemen said, "We'll
give you a ride home. We're going that way."

"This your dog? He can
come along, too."
Marathon wagged his tail.
The policeman ruffled his fur.

So they drove home in the police car to Steve's apartment,
and the policemen helped Steve up the stairs.

Steve and Marathon stayed home for two days,
but Steve's foot was no better.

Marathon was taken for little strolls along the
sidewalk by the girl who lived across the hall,
and that was all.

Finally Steve called the doctor.

He came, and looked at Steve's foot. "Ah, a
strained tendon. You haven't been jogging by
any chance, have you?"

"Yes," said Steve proudly. "I run every day—sometimes twice a day."

"Ah, suspected as much," said the doctor, shaking his head. "No more running, not on these roads."

"But how will I keep in shape?" asked Steve.

"Ever thought about swimming?" asked the doctor, bandaging up Steve's ankle. "No jarring of the joints, no straining of the tendons—best exercise in the world. Swimming pool just down the road. Try that."

When he had gone, Steve took Marathon's face in his hands. Steve was close to tears. Marathon's tail wagged.

"I won't be able to take you to the pool. Poor Marathon, no more runs. How will you manage?"

Marathon's tail wagged even harder. He had a pretty good idea.

So from that day on, every time Steve went
swimming, Marathon guarded the apartment.
Steve left the television on for him so that he
would not feel lonely...

and brought him back
a package of potato
chips from the pool.

And sometimes he'd say, "Bad luck, Marathon,
no run. But I'll just take you out for a minute,"
and they would go for a little stroll past the shops.

And in the summer they both went to the seaside.
Steve swam, and Marathon ran in and out of the
waves and barked and fetched sticks.

I am a real dog after all, he thought,
smiling from ear to ear.